Well Don~~~~~~

An Ivy and Mack story

Written by Rebecca Colby
Illustrated by Gustavo Mazali
with Szépvölgyi Eszter

Collins

What's in this story?

Listen and say

Sports Day

children

race

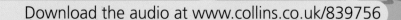

egg

spoon

Sports Day

4

Mack says, "Croc loves Sports Day, too. And Mum and Dad!"

Mack says, "Look, Croc!
Ivy is throwing the ball."

Mack is clapping. Mum and Dad are clapping.

Mack says, "Well done, Ivy! You're great!"

Mack and Croc are running.
Ivy says, "Run, Mack, run!"

His family are clapping.
Ivy says, "Hooray for Mack!"

Mack says, "Ivy is jumping. Wow! That is VERY good!"

Her family are clapping again.
Mack says, "Ivy is great!"

Ivy asks, "Where are Mack and Croc? Are they hopping?"

Ivy says, "Hop, Mack, hop!"

It's the egg and spoon race. Ivy is walking with her egg and spoon.

Mack says, "Go, Ivy, go!"

Oh no! The egg ...

... FALLS!

Mack says, "Get the egg! Get the egg! Don't stop!"

Ivy looks at the children.
Ivy says, "Oh no!"

Mack says, "You LOVE Sports Day.
Please finish, Ivy!"

Ivy listens to Mack. She gets the egg.

Ivy says, "You're right, Mack. I love Sports Day!"

21

Picture dictionary

Listen and repeat

clapping

hopping

jumping

running

throwing

walking

1 Look and order the story

2 Listen and say

Collins

Published by Collins
An imprint of HarperCollins*Publishers*
Westerhill Road
Bishopbriggs
Glasgow
G64 2QT

William Collins' dream of knowledge for all began with the publication of his first book in 1819.

A self-educated mill worker, he not only enriched millions of lives, but also founded a flourishing publishing house. Today, staying true to this spirit, Collins books are packed with inspiration, innovation and practical expertise. They place you at the centre of a world of possibility and give you exactly what you need to explore it.

10 9 8 7 6 5 4 3 2 1

ISBN 978-0-00-839756-2

Collins® and COBUILD® are registered trademarks of HarperCollins*Publishers* Limited

www.collins.co.uk/elt

British Library Cataloguing in Publication Data

A catalogue record for this publication is available from the British Library.

Author: Rebecca Colby
Lead Illustrator: Gustavo Mazali (Beehive)
Copy Artist: Szépvölgyi Eszter (Beehive)
Series editor: Rebecca Adlard
Publishing manager: Lisa Todd
Product managers: Jennifer Hall and Caroline Green
In-house editor: Alma Puts Keren
Project manager: Emily Hooton
Editor: Deborah Friedland
Proofreaders: Natalie Murray and Michael Lamb
Cover designer: Kevin Robbins
Typesetter: 2Hoots Publishing Services Ltd
Audio produced by id audio, London
Reading guide author: Julie Penn
Production controller: Rachel Weaver
Printed and bound by: GPS Group, Slovenia

MIX
Paper from
responsible sources
FSC™ C007454

This book is produced from independently certified FSC™ paper to ensure responsible forest management.

For more information visit: **www.harpercollins.co.uk/green**

Download the audio for this book and a reading guide for parents and teachers at www.collins.co.uk/839756